# The Tiptoe Guide to Tracking Fairies

by Ammi-Joan Paquette    illustrated by Christa Unzner

Tanglewood · Terre Haute, IN

Design by Amy Alick Perich

Tanglewood Publishing, Inc.
4400 Hulman Street
Terre Haute, IN 47803
www.tanglewoodbooks.com

Printed in the United States of America, WOR/FEB 2011. First printing.
10 9 8 7 6 5 4 3 2 1

ISBN 978-1-933718-50-7


Library of Congress Cataloging-in-Publication Data

Paquette, Ammi-Joan.
    The tiptoe guide to tracking fairies / by Ammi-Joan Paquette ; illustrated by Christa Unzner.
        p. cm.
    Summary: Takes the reader on a journey to look for signs of fairies living nearby, from hiding places in tulips to a lookout post in a tree.
    ISBN 978-1-933718-20-0
    [1. Fairies--Fiction. 2. Imagination--Fiction. 3. Nature--Fiction.]   I. Unzner-Fischer, Christa, ill. II. Title.
    PZ7.P2119Tip 2009
    [E]--dc22
                                                2008042792

for Kim and Lauren,
my original fairy Crackers
- AJP


for Thea
- CU

Some people think that fairies only live far away in magical lands. Many fairies do. But there are some fairies, a few, who live all around us. We can see where they live if we know how to look for them.

The sun is shining, and we are in the mood for adventure. It's a perfect day for tracking fairies! Let's go look for clues.

Fairies love flowers. These tulips would be just right for playing hide-and-seek. Curled up inside, a fairy could not be spotted by anyone.

Something is twinkling! Is that a fairy's lost slipper? We'll put it on this rock, so she can find it again.

Under a tiny waterfall, fairies might bathe on a hot summer night and then stretch out and dry their wings by the light of the moon.

We moved a big rock to make a pool
that will be just right for splashing
and diving. We hope they find it!

Here's a little hideout! A fairy has made a soft bed in here, with pine needles tucked under a wide green leaf.

This dandelion fluff will be just right for a pillow. Sleep well, hidden fairies!

What are these? Acorn shells! Some fairies have been very busy gathering acorns and hollowing them out. With the tender acorn meat, fairies can make their favorite dessert: sweet acorn mousse.

Maybe the fairies would like
this treat to add to their feast!

Hello, little chipmunk! Have you seen any fairies around?

Fairies love to play with chipmunks, but only the bravest dare try the most exciting sport of all: bareback riding. The chipmunk bucks and leaps, but skilled fairies can stay on and on.

These nuts will keep the chipmunk still for a minute. Maybe one of the slower fairies will have a chance to sneak up and catch a ride.

Now we have come to the heart of the forest: the ring of fairy trees. A tree planted by fairies grows from seed to sapling in just a few weeks. When the young trees bud and blossom, we know that fairies are not far away.

But where can they be?

Do you see this? It must be a
LOOKOUT post!

Yes, fairies have kept watch for
intruders from up here. One low
whistle and…

Swish! Every winged partygoer slips behind
a rock, under a plant, or inside a flower, pulling
the petals shut behind her.

Waiting. Just waiting for someone to pass by.
Maybe you and me!

We have followed all their clues and looked
in all their hiding spots. But those fairies
are too tricky for us. We will have to
come back and try again another day.

Wait! Did you feel that tingle? I think
something magical is about to happen.

What are all those petals on the ground?
It looks like a message.

Is it from the fairies?